PIAOTT Publishing and Graphic Design LLC, Chicago, IL

My Brothers In Christ

Shirley Rice and Wilma Brumfield-Lofton

Printed in the United States of America

©2021 by Library of Congress Cataloging-in-Publication Data

ISBN: 978-1-7362522-6-0

I0618277

My Brothers In Christ

Author
Shirley Rice

Co-Author
Wilma Brumfield-Lofton

Table of Contents

A message from the authors.

"My Brothers in Christ" represents men from all walks of life, fathers, sons, grandfathers, brothers, uncles, nephews, and cousins. Pastors, teachers, coaches, deacons, laymen, mentors, counselors, health care workers, singers, and frontline workers and so many workers. These men are the movers and shakers of the world. Men making a difference as they impact the lives of others. My prayers are that everyone who reads this book will bear in mind that God is still working through those who remain faithful to him.

These men are real men who stand up for Jesus. As you read this book ask God to help you make a difference in the life of our young adults. Especially our young males to lift those who have fallen. Real men lead by example and are a blessing to others wherever they go. They often look for an opportunity to make the lives of their brothers so much better.

Are they perfect? No of course not! No man is perfect. Only our Load and Savior Jesus Christ is perfect. He is the one who committed no sin. Yet he was bruised, beaten, stabbed, and stoned. He left a road map for us to follow "THE BIBLE"

My prayer remain that men bless their children and other men related or unrelated. "Each one teach one as you reach one" "Iron Sharpen Iron" Help the children and young adult males by supplying their needs. "Charity suffereth long and is kind, charity envieth not; Charity vaunteth not itself, is not puffed up." I Corinthians 13:4

Shirley Rice

These stories are very inspiring. Men showing brotherly love and kindness. Always there for each other doing the good times or bad, during the highs and the lows. Always there to help you through whatever situation you may be going through. Ready to lend a helping hand or encouraging word. Laugh together and cry together. Someone you can share your everyday experiences and one who accepts your worst, but will help you to become your best! It's a blessing to have loyal, devoted, thoughtful loving Brothers In Christ, praying for each other and lifting each other. Mark 12: 30-31

Wilma Brumfield-Lofton

Pastor Alfonso Boone

"It is incredible what God would do."

Sometimes, God put people in your path to be a blessing to, or for them to be a blessing to you, so it is with my brother Elder Moses Anderson, Jr.

I met this young man while he was a game warden and State Trooper for Florida. He was also the pastor of a small church in Frostproof, FL. I had never heard of this town before, but the Lord made a connection that bonded us for life. As time went by, the revivals I did every year at the church reached the masses, and many souls were set free and delivered. As we spent time together, the friendship became stronger and stronger and has lasted for more than thirty years. Our friendship bonded our families together, and to this day, his children call me

ELDER MOSES ANDERSON JR.

"Papa." I have watched his children grow up and saw the grandchildren arrive and grow up, and I love each one of them. As I affectionately call him, Mo loves people and shares his love with everyone he meets regardless of color, race, or creed. Because of this, the Lord has blessed him abundantly. He was able to leave the game warden and sheriff jobs and become an entrepreneur.

It is incredible what God would do when you lend yourself to him. He was blessed with his own construction business, daycare, a bible bookstore, and many other businesses. He also owned an orange grove, and God gave him favor among many prominent farmers along the way. Because of this, I have been able to witness nature in the raw. He took me places such as where he worked as a game warden to the eagle sanctuary. I have seen large crocodiles up close, and through it all, the Lord keeps blessing my brother and friend, who has helped me out on so many occasions.

I recall one story, my wife and I had to catch a cruise ship in Fort Lauderdale. He drove so fast from Avon park, where he lives, trying to get us there that the state trooper stopped him. The trooper asked, "Mr. Anderson, where are you going in such a hurry?" After much explaining, he begged him to slow down. We made it there in one piece, and it was so early that we went into the ship and had to come out and return in when it was boarding time.

Mo loves his family, and he loves his church, where he pastors the House Of Praise Church Of God By Faith in Frostproof, FL. He also loves the people that God has entrusted him with to shepherd. Mo and I have weathered lots of storms with our families and the church. We have cried together, talked closely together, and still kept our dignity. And through it all, we stood tall, the friendship grew stronger, and we are still running for the Lord together.

Mo is a true brother and friend. And there are many things I can say about him. He had good cars and bad cars but traveled the highways and stayed faithful to God. His faithfulness has made him an adjutant on the National Board of Church Of God By Faith. He supports the Bishop Board and works with all the Superintendents. Even in doing all this, Mo makes time to take good care of his Mom and Dad.

We still check on each other, and even though we have been apart for the past three years, we still do not miss a beat to make sure that each other is doing well. If you are anywhere around Avon Park or Frostproof, FL, ask for Pastor Moses Anderson. He will make sure that you are well taken care of, "Royalty Style." I am proud to know such a man who is loyal, loving, and trustworthy. I pray that God continues to richly bless him and his loving wife Delores as they continue to bless God's people and stay faithful to each other.

> *Proverbs 18:24 "A man that hath friends must show himself friendly; and there is a friend that sticketh closer than a brother."*

PASTOR BOONE AND ELDER GREEN

Well, what can I say about my friend, Elder Herbert Green Jr. I met him in the early seventies around nineteen seventy-three or four. I was a teenager and a Minister, and my family had just moved to Georgia. He was Pastoring in Winterpark, Florida, and had a strong influence on my sister June, who was a member of his church at that time. She had talked so much about him that I thought he was about six feet tall. When I met him, I found out he was "all of" five feet tall but packed a powerful punch. After talking with him, he became a great mentor, brother, and friend and is affectionately called "the short man."

The thing that gets you on meeting "the short man" is that he is mighty and strong in wisdom and faith even though short in stature. He was the father of seven children; four of them have since passed. I watched him stand there and preached their funerals. When his first wife passed, I watched him in sorrow but stood tall. He was physically blind, but he stood tall and walked his faith through, and because he kept the faith, God restored his eyesight.

I follow him because of his faith in God. He was on the National Examining Board for Ministers. He is the head man of the Superintendents Board, on the Trustee Board of the Churches Of God By Faith, the Overseer of the South Florida District, and faithfully shepherds his flock in Winterhaven, Florida. There is nothing he would not do to help the church, his members, or anyone around him. As he examined men, including me, one of the most incredible things I heard him say was, "You cannot treat people like cargo. You must be pure in spirit and heart." As he examined men, he was not impressed so much by their skill and ability, but he looked for their spirit and their heart to see if they were worthy of leading God's people.

As our relationship grew, he not only became a mentor and a mentee but, we became very good friends. Our children grew up together, and he walked me through some dark times. He was there through my father's, my two sisters', and my mother's death, and I stood with him through his troubled times. We have traveled across the country together doing workshops in Kansas City, MS; Memphis, TN; Tacoma, WA; Detroit, MI; Long Island, NY; Newark, NJ; and wherever there was a church to be planted, Elder Green would go, and we went together and did great exploits for the Lord, yes; the scripture in Proverbs says: there is a friend that sticks closer than a brother, and a man that has a friend must show himself friendly, and it definitely fits my brother my friend Elder. Herbert Green, Jr.

Today, we are still holding on and staying in contact, even though I am in Newark, NJ; and he is in Winter Haven, FL. We have come up through the ranks and serve as Chairman and Vice-Chairman of the Superintendents board and the Trustee board that helps the National Executive Council of the Churches Of God By Faith. It has indeed been a great experience serving alongside such a fine man and growing together with him. I pray that God will allow us to continue to grow together until our race is finished. May God continues to bless him and his wife Cathy with good health is my prayer.

Proverbs 19:17 says: "Whoever is generous to the poor lends to the Lord, and he will repay him for his deed."

HAL TROTTER

What can I say about my son/friend Hal? I said it like that because he is married to my little girl Nell who has been with us for 40 plus years. Us, meaning my wife and me, who adopted her, and she keeps up with us every day. My daughter has many fun stories, but I am here to talk of her husband, Hal.

I met Hal in March 2017, when he and my daughter were talking about getting married. I found him to be a gentle giant. All six feet plus of him is quiet in speech and full of knowledge. When we lived in Memphis, they would visit when they knew we had something at the church. On December 23rd, 2017, we drove to Union, MS, and it was my great pleasure to join him and my daughter in Holy Matrimony. It was a beautiful ceremony and a joy to be in his presence.

Hal takes care of the Ministry of Freed N' Deed in Union, MS. He cares so much for the little babies that he makes a round trip of sixty miles to pick them up, feed them, clothe them, and teach them God's word. I know this is very commendable because it is done with such patience. I rode with him on one occasion. He started at about five o'clock making that trip, then when church service is over about seven or eight, he gets them all on the bus and takes them back home. That night I rode with him. I prayed God's blessings upon him because he was so gracious in all of it. I think we made it back home about midnight, and he does this every Monday unless he has taken a break.

I recall so many stories. When we moved to New Jersey, he and my daughter visited with us and came to church. He even made it possible for his babies to travel to different places and enjoy something different. Hal took his babies to Ohio and Kentucky to see Noah's Ark, the Creation Museum, and the Aquarium, and I wish I had the pictures to show you real love. Not only did he take them, but he invited my wife and blessed her with the best vacation. They took her to see her favorite Pastor in Baton Rouge, LA, Pastor Jimmy Swaggart. She came back saying it was the best vacation she ever had because it was topped off with seeing her Pastor shaking his hands and talking with him.

I love him. One time, the church roof was leaking, and water was running like Niagara Falls. He was pumping, sweeping, and mopping, and through the stress of it, he does it all without complaining. His patience is such a light not only to me but to others and the ministry. He loves children, and he loves his grandchildren. He loves people unconditionally. He does not beg but gives because he has a love of God within. I thank God for my son/friend Hal, and I pray God continues to provide him with the strength to do all that he desires to do.

A prayer for my son/friend:

Almighty God, I entrust Hal, who is dear to me, into your never-failing care and love, for this life and the life to come—knowing that you will do for him better things than I can desire or pray through Jesus Christ our Lord. Lord, please give my treasured friend love and blessings without end. Amen

I love you, my son/friend.

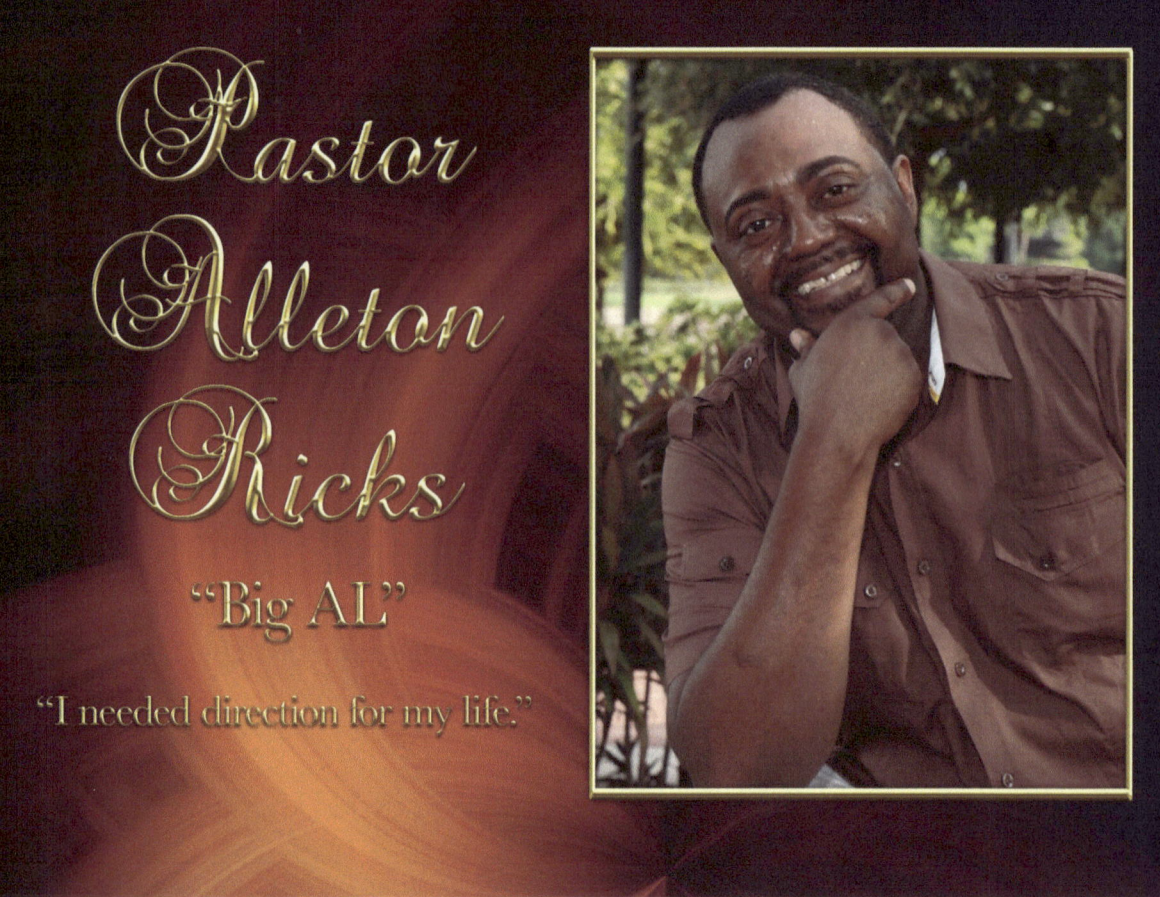

Pastor Alleton Ricks

"Big AL"

"I needed direction for my life."

The Lord has blessed me with two Men of God that I can say have a significant impact on my life: Prophet Vanskie Montaie and Bishop Clint Brown. Before rededicating my life to the Lord, I struggled with drugs which ended with a divorce. In 1994, I went to rehab, where I gave my life to the Lord and immediately remarried and rejoined my family. We attended church regularly, and I stayed off drugs for over two years until I relapsed. We moved and attended Covenant Ministries Church, where Bishop Anna Aytch taught us the adeptness Word of God. Here is where I met Prophet Vanskie Montaie and heard the testimony of his drug struggle and deliverance. I knew at that moment what I was missing is being completely delivered from drugs. He announced that he was having a deliverance service, but I was scheduled to work. My wife went to the service while I was at work. My Supervisor walked up to me and informed me that I did not need to work over; therefore, I drove to the service. When I walked in and sat beside my wife, Prophet Montaie called me to come to him. He asked his armor-bearer to go to his car and bring him a suit. He told me that God told him to bring the suit to a man who was going to be completely delivered from drugs and that the suit would fit me without any tailoring. He took the jacket, put it on me, praying for deliverance over my body. The suit fitted me exactly as he stated, and I have been off drugs ever since that night.

In 2001, we moved to Florida and lost contact with Prophet Montaie until last year; God Blessed us to come together again. We

have been under Bishop Clint Brown since 2001. Bishop Brown gave my wife and I the push to move into ministry over couples. He ordained us to be who God purposed us to be. As I have watched his struggles, his praise, his worship, and his push, it drives me more and keeps me striving to be who God purposed me to be as a Man of God. Helping and Blessing couples keeps me focusing more on ministering to family's togetherness and equipping couples to be married for a lifetime God's way. Bishop Brown taught me what Praise and Worship truly is. I honor these two Men of God! They are more than friends to me; they are my FAMILY and My Brothers In Christ!

Pastor Antwon Brown

Greetings brothers and sisters of the Most High God. I pray this finds you in perfect peace. My name is Antwon Brown, I am the pastor of the Liberty Baptist Church of Gary, Indiana. I am married to a lovely lady by the name of Jennifer and together we have 3 sons. (Josiah, Joshua, and Joseph) I count it all joy and a privilege to express my love for brothers everywhere, and of every race and creed. I believe in the power of unity. As a pastor and youth AAU basketball coach I strongly believe in TEAM. When I was young boy, I was always told that team is spelled T E A M and that the acronym for team is Together Everyone Achieves More. My prayer daily is that men come together in unity. I genuinely believe coming together as a team is the only way to combat the evilness of this world. For the bible teaches us in 1 Corinthians 12:12-27 that we are many parts, yet we are one body. Paul encourages us, letting us know that the body only functions properly when its parts are working TOGETHER. If our schools are going to get better, if our streets are going to become safe again, if our neighborhoods are going to become drug free, if our nation is going to be healed, men must come together in UNITY. I want to do this as I close. I want to thank each and every man reading this focused on making a positive difference. I thank you and thank God for your service and your sacrifice. Keep up the good work but most important keep God your focus. Let's move forward together.

"Shout Team on Me, Shout Team on Three, 1, 2, 3 ((TEAM!!!))"

Bobbie Ray Stubblefield Jr.

My name is Bobbie Ray Stubblefield, Sr. I was born November 1, 1959, to Bennie Bob and Mary Stubblefield. I am the baby of twelve children raised on a small farm in Delhi, Louisiana. We all picked cot-ton had a truck patch (garden). My father taught us all about hard work. My mother taught us how important education was. She said, "If you can read, you can understand the Bible." My mother made sure we all went to church and understood the Bible. My mother was a true Christian. On the farm, we had an outhouse, well water, and a wooden stove. God provided us with all we needed. We came from the outhouse to an in-house bathroom, from well water to running water, and from a wood stove to central heating. The family was not ashamed because if it was good enough for my parents, it was good for the family. We all loved our parents and respected their wishes. At the age of 17, I graduated from high school and instantly went into the Army. That's when I faded away from my Christian faith. At the age of 21, I married my first wife, and we conceived a son four years later. This marriage lasted 22 years; I was lost. Then I went back to church and let my Heavenly Father take my life into his hands again. My Heavenly Father makes no mistake. I met my current wife in 2004, and I have been blessed ever since. Family is one of God's gifts today. In all things, put God first, and everything will work out for good. Given honor to Pastor Antwon Brown and Minster Shirley Rice for their leadership and faith. Liberty Baptist Church is where my faith grows, and I praise my Heavenly Father.

Minister Brandon Moore

"Their support never wavered..."

It does not take long for me to think of who my brothers are. For 25 plus years, these men have had my back at every turbulent time and triumphant moment. The one that sticks is when my calling was becoming stronger on me, and I finally accepted it. I called them and said, hey, I need to sit down and tell you something. After opening up and telling them the change that I was going through, they simply said, we were just waiting for you to tell us when. We always knew. Their support has never wavered, and the love between us only grows. These brothers are my keepers, and I am theirs. For this, I am ever grateful to have them in my life. They Are My Brothers In Christ!

Pastor Carlos Orr

"I am blessed and grateful..."

I am Pastor Carlos Orr, the pastor of Greater Ebenezer M.B. Church in Aberdeen, MS. My wife is the lovely first lady Deborah, we have been married for 17 years. We have 4 children and 7 grandchildren. I am blessed and grateful to have loyal dedicated members and strong godly men who are very devoted. These caring, giving members of the brotherhood ministry are committed to praying for and helping others. They are My Brothers In Christ.

JAMES LENOIR
TRUSTEE PRESIDENT

THE MEN OF GREATER EBENEZER M.B. CHURCH
CHAIRMAN DEACON-RANDY DOSS
DEACON JIMMY PARGO, DEACON WILLIE MCMILLIAN, DEACON ROYCE STEPHENSON,
DEACON EDDIE HOSKINS, DEACON RICHARD JONES, DEACON RICKY FAIR

Minister Don Morgan

"I am known as the Cowboy Preacher"

I was born and raised in Belmount Missionary Baptist Church in Millington, Tennessee. Around the latter portion of 2010, I left Belmount because of things that happened under past leadership. The new Pastor contacted me and told me all the things he had planned for our ministry and the healing of our community. I was broken, disappointed and decided not to come back to church. The new Pastor kept calling me, ministering to me, and showing me Christian love in abundance. I began to be filled with anticipation for the calls. It took Pastor Patterson 2 or 3 years before he earned my trust. He never gave up on me. The Pastor kept calling me until the Lord changed my heart, and I returned to the church. It felt like fire in my bones. The Lord Jesus Christ called me to preach his gospel and spread the good news. My love affair with the Master became stronger and stronger under Pastor's leadership. My Pastor became my mentor and

closest friend. We talk all the time, and I love our conversations. I never had a friend like Pastor Patterson; it is best described as a Paul and Silas situation. Belmount Missionary Baptist Church has the best leader ever right now, a little country

PASTOR MORRIS PATTERSON

church 121 years old this year with a Shepherd who walks it as he talks it. It makes me joyful to come to the house of worship because I just love it. All week long, I look forward to prayer, testimony, and worship on Sunday.

My relationship is super tight with my righteous spiritual brother, and our closeness is a gospel blessing of the Lord. Praise God for my Pastor, Morris Patterson. He is genuinely My Brother In Christ.

Elijah Taylor

"My brother's consistent encouragement and belief in me..."

I grew up in Charleston, Mississippi, in a Christian home. My parents Daisy and Ben Taylor, were both Christians. On Sundays, my parents, siblings, and I would attend Sunday School, Sunday Worship, and Evening Service. I used to sing in the choir and was baptized at the age of 13 Years old.

When I graduated from high school, I moved to Milwaukee, Wisconsin. After arriving in Milwaukee, I attended church a couple of Sundays with my brother. Once I start going out to the clubs and having a good time partying etc. I stopped attending church, started drinking and doing worldly things, and had fallen away from the

PASTOR OLLIE TAYLOR

church. I left Milwaukee and lived in several other states. I moved to New York, Atlanta, Memphis, Illinois, and Iowa. Later, when I moved back to Milwaukee, my brother would constantly ask me, "when are you coming back to church?" Finally, I started visiting off and on for about a year.

Then I decided to join and become a member and get back to serving the Lord. I attended an AA Class while living in Memphis, TN. I am very proud to say that I completely gave up alcohol and drugs. My brother was happy that I finally became a Good Hope M.B. Church member, where he is the Pastor and his wife Sandra is the First Lady. My brother's consistent encouragement and belief in me helped transform me into the christian I am today. He gave me a key to the church I would clean up during the week, cut the grass during the spring and summer months, and Shovel snow during the winter months. I would be there Sunday mornings to open up the church for our Sunday morning Worship Experience. My brother Pastor Ollie Taylor is a blessing to me, and that is why I name him "My Brother In Christ."

Pastor Gary Sheldon

"I needed direction for my life."

There is so much to say about a man who is a Father, a brother, and a friend. It has been over 30 years now since I met Pastor Boone. It was at Breakthrough Church of God By Faith when I needed direction for my life. Over the years, he has helped me in so many ways: my marriage, manhood, and ministry. If there has been one thing that has stood out to me about him is his love for people, I mean all people.

I have seen him at his highest and lowest times, but he has continued to stand strong in faith and serve in the Kingdom. I know that there is nothing I cannot share with him, and have I shared lol. But regardless of the conversation, he has never looked or treated me any different.

The Lord gave me Pastor Boone because he knew he would be for me at this time in my life just what I needed. I appreciate and will always Love and Respect him for being the example he has been. To others, he is Pastor, Superintendent, or National Board member, but my brother in Christ is "Pop," and I am his Son.

PASTOR ALFONSO BOONE

The Greens

RUSSELL GREEN

We are Anthony, Kenny, Russell Jr., and Ramone. We are proud to talk about our dad Russell Green who we call pop. As we grew from boys to men, thinking of someday that we would become fathers as well. We are thankful that we have a great example to follow. We love our dad so much we appreciate all the hugs, kisses, handshakes, and wise advice. Even the spankings making us stronger and responsible for our mistakes. Dad taught us how to defend ourselves, be respectful also to love each other. Thank you, pop! We enjoy our best friend, our Brother In Christ, our pop who is always there to listen to our problems and give us great advice. You became a man at a young age with a family after you married our beautiful mother Juanita, and we know it was not easy raising 4 sons and being a husband. We did not have a lot, but we had all we needed. We are wealthy with love because of you and mom showing us so much love. You always told us, "If anything happens to me, y'all take care of mom, and y'all love and take care of each other." Your words have carried on through the families we have now! We want you to know this now because life is short! Pop words cannot explain the love, loyalty, and respect we have for you. We will love you, respect you and protect you always your 4 grateful sons.

Hugh Leavell

"My Brothers!"

My story is not unique in itself, and I am not by any means special or better, at least not in the most common sense. I can't tell it all (this book would be about me), but I'll give you a glimpse into my life. Here's my story. At a very young age, I had to go to church. My father was a deacon, and my mother, an Eastern Star. One of the benefits of me being who I am. I will get to that part later. Anyway, we had to go to church. Practically every time the church doors open, we were there. Not only did we have to go to church, but we were also given a briefing before we got out of the car. No talking, no sleeping, no eating, and sit still. This was my initial experience with church. To me, it was very boring. I mean, we were like robots. It was a Southern Baptist church out in the middle of the woods. The songs were boring, the preaching was boring, and we had to sit there. In particular, there was nothing special, but it was my introduction to church and Christ.

In my early childhood, the first thing we did in school was learn the Lord's Prayer and pledge allegiance to the flag every day. Knowing the Lord's Prayer in school was another part of my introduction to the church. It started at home and then carried over in school. The training that I received in both places was not enough to sustain me from riotous living. That also came a little later. I suppose we were giving everything they knew to give us concerning the church. Sex was not included in either environment. A little later for that too.

The one benefit that has carried me throughout my life was the discipline I received at home. Mom and dad were very strict. They taught me discipline and instilled in me values and character traits that have span my entire life. They taught me things like fatherhood, honor, respect, honesty, how to sit at a table, work habits, blessing your food before you eat, eating as a family, say yes ma'am/sir and no ma'am/sir. It was the little things that have carried me throughout my life and have made me a better man. These traits were the foundation of my becoming a man and instill these same disciplines and qualities in my children.

Growing up in a small town in Kentucky, we did not have much. We were poor. We just did not know we were poor because everyone around us was poor. There is one thing that still holds true; we never needed anything. Everything we needed was always there. I have never gone hungry or without shelter or clothes. My wants were a bit different. The only time I can remember getting what I wanted was at Christmas. My parents went the extra mile when it came to Christmas and getting us what we wanted. I knew at a young age that Santa Claus was not real. But my parents wanted us to believe in that myth for some reason. I remember getting a whooping for peeping around the refrigerator on Christmas Eve, but that's another story.

Oh, by the way, we did not get timeouts, spankings, or let me talk to you; we got whoopings—something else I carried into my manhood. Did I mention teachers, principals, superintendents, other family members, neighbors, and just about anyone could whoop you? As long as they told mom and dad why they whooped you, it was okay. But you got another whooping when you got home.

As a young boy, I do not remember doing any work inside the house until I was around 11 or so. The boys worked outside. I had to slop the pigs, empty the night pot, feed the chickens, cut the grass, work in the garden and do anything outside that needed doing. You ask, what is a night pot? A night pot is what you sat on at night when you had to use the bathroom. It was a porcelain pot; some people called them slop johns. Go figure. We didn't have a bathroom in the house. We had an outhouse. I was about 9 or 10 when we finally got an in-house bathroom. It was heaven. What does this have to do about anything? Actually everything.

When you can appreciate the small things, you are in a better position to appreciate bigger things. I have never forgotten my upbringing. The man that I am is because of my upbringing. My parents loved me and instilled in me the disciplines that I still hold true to my heart at a very young age. The most significant part of my manhood is my youth. I was not perfect, not an angel, but I had character. My entire life has been based on the character traits instilled in me as a child. One of my biggest regrets was not being taught about sex. The need for sex is natural, and we were simply told not to do it. It instigated a sense of wonder.

When I was 16, one of my childhood sweethearts was pregnant with my first child. At the age of 17, 2 girls were pregnant at the same time. Can you imagine being 17 and having two children on the way? I was a senior in high school with no meaningful job, but I had a sense of responsibility. Daddy always said, "If you're man enough to make a baby, be man enough to take care of it." So, I threw myself into manhood, and I didn't have a clue. I dismissed my dreams of being an electrical engineer and traded them for a rifle. I joined the military, the Army. No one pushed or told me to do this. It was a self-made decision based

on the disciplines that had been instilled in me. I had a mother and father, and no child of mine would not grow up without me actively being a part of their lives.

I did not finish my senior year of high school; I dropped out. At 17, I joined the military solely to take care of my children. I did not know what I was doing at the time, but I just knew I had to do something quickly, and that was the quickest way I knew. I had three older brothers who had joined the Army, so that might have impacted my decision. I have only seen my father cry three times in my life. The first was when he thought he had lost his paycheck. I was about 8. He came home from work and could not find his paycheck. Momma did not know what to think, and daddy just couldn't find it. Remember, we were poor. Every penny mattered. That evening he sat at the kitchen table and had tears running down his face. He stood up, took off his coveralls, and the check fell on the floor. I had tears of joy. He wiped his eyes and gave the check to momma.

The second time I saw him cry was when I asked him to sign the papers to emancipate me so I could join the Army. I explained why and he reluctantly signed the papers and had tears running down his face. The third time was when I returned home thirteen weeks later after completing my advanced training. I went to his job with my uniform on. As I walked towards him, he did not know who I was, and he started walking towards me. When he recognizes who I was, I started running towards him, and we hugged for a long time. When he released me, he had tears running down his face and said, "The Army is making a man out of you." I said, no, they are just making me eat a lot. When I joined the Army, I weighed 107 pounds. After advance training, I weighed 134. It was moments like that I appreciated the most. I knew I was loved, and I wanted to give my children that same love. I have more, but I have to get out of Kentucky. I could stay here and write about this all day. I can't tell it all in such a small space. Let's go to Germany.

My first duty assignment was in Germany. At 17, I was in another country. Young, dumb, and naive to the ways of the world. I was placed in an environment of sex, drugs, alcohol, death, crime, war, spies, and a world where no laws existed, at least for us. We could do anything, anytime, and it seemed like nothing was wrong with it. I joined the military after the Vietnam War, and life was different. This little boy from Kentucky now had to make life and death decisions. Sometimes I chose wrong, and sometimes I got it right. As a soldier we were untouchable, at least that's what we thought. Everyone was beneath us. We ruled the world, at least the country. I was in awe of everything that was coming at me at the speed of light. I knew the church, but it was not enough. I went to the chapel, but the chaplain could not deliver the Sunday message like I was used to, so it did not help. I just kept on growing up and living a life of everything that went against what I knew was right. I was not that far gone, but I encountered some bad life experiences. At the same time, it helped make me the man I am. I can not tell you all that I encountered. You probably would not believe it. Let's move on.

My Uncle Charlie passed away, and I came home on emergency leave. When I got home, I reunited with one of my childhood sweethearts, and in two weeks, we were married. She had two children (2 and 3) that were not mine, so now I had four children. It was different, but it settled me down and took me back to the roots of who I was. I went to her church, and for the first time, I experience God like never before. I was made to go to church as a child. Made to get baptized, but I didn't know God for myself. Bishop Alphonso Scott, the Lively Stone Apostolic Church pastor in Nortonville, Kentucky, preached a sermon. It was about the young man who had taken his inheritance and lived a life of riotous living and then returned home. He was talking about me. Talking to me, and did not know who I was. When the altar call was given, I ran down to the altar, got re-baptized in the Name of Jesus, came up out of the water speaking in tongues, and my life has never been the same. God was preparing me for something.

After that experience or encounter with God, I had a yearning, burning desire to know who Jesus was. I learn to talk to God and not at him. To pray to him without asking for anything. I had a hunger and thirst for knowledge. I began this journey of seeking, searching, and never being satisfied. That hunger and thirst still exist today. I am running out of space, so I have to bring this to a close. Since my first actual encounter with Jesus at the age of 20, He has been directing my life. I've made a lot of mistakes and continue to make mistakes. I'm not perfect but knowing who Jesus is and what he represents makes this life worth living even more. God is not looking for perfection; He is looking for consistency, sincerity, honesty, respect, and acknowledgment. Oh, those same character traits that my parents instilled in me when I was a child. May God bless whomever these words may reach and remember, when you return home, there's going to be a party. You figure it out.

I can not leave it there. There are voids in this excerpt that I don't have the space to tell. God did allow me to get my GED at the age of 18, associate degree in Liberal Arts with a concentration on business, bachelor's degree in Radio, Television, and Film, bachelor's degree in Journalism, and a master's degree in Public Relations. I retired from active duty after 21 years of service. I currently work for the federal government as a public affairs specialist. In addition to that, I mentor teenagers to instill fundamental values, and I own my own video production company.

Sky Productions Video
https://www.skypvideo.com.

Jerome Spencer

"One hot summer night..."

In August of 1973, Reverend Clarence Bailey had a dream that he was the Manager of a gospel group dressed in all white, singing on stage. The following day, he decided to chase his dream and make it come to reality.

He began to recruit former member of different groups in and out of church. Reverend Bailey called Jerome (Ronnie) Spencer, former member of Spirit of Harmony to assist. Jerome graciously agreed to help. He called Mr. Henry (Goat) Hill, former lead singer of the Gospel Choice and Comic Energy (Night Club Group). Brother Hill recruited Willie (Cat) Thomas and Johnnie Woods, both popular musicians.

Then, It was time to get the remaining background singers together. Brother Hill suggested we call Charles (Chuck) Jones, Don (Won) Padget and Michael (Mike) Williams. They were all former members of the Sounds of Glory. Lastly, we heard of a Drum Teacher named Ronald (Skeet) Davis.

The group began to practice two days per week. Shortly after, on August 8, 1973, Reverend Bailey announced that the "Southern Jubilees" were born. Praise God from whom all blessings flow.

We purchased all White Tuxedos with long tails and Top Hats. Reverend Bailey started booking the group on various programs in and out of the city along with supporting Chicago musicals. We began to get recognized and the group put together a Major Program using The Jackson Southern Aires as the drawing card at the Babe Youth Center in Gary, Indiana. Our motto was, "If I could just make it on in," Shortly after that, we were asked by the Mighty Clouds of Joy to open their Musical at the Hammond Civic Center. The group was traveling in and out of the state singing every weekend. We decided (by the grace of God) to go into the studio and cut our 1st single entitled, "Vow," a Promise to the Lord written by Brother Hill.

The group continued to sing on many engagements. We were often called, "The Gospel Temptations." Three (3) of our major players of the group was called home and the Southern Jubilees began singing less. We still make singing engagements at our member's churches.

SOUTHERN JUBILEES

Rev. Clarence Bailey
Booking Manager & Founder

Brother Chuck Jones
1st Tenor

Elder Henry Hill
Lead Singer

Brother Don Padget
2nd Tenor

Brother Jerome Spencer
Baritone

Brother Mike Williams
Base Singer

Musicians:
Brother Willie Thomas
Lead Guitar and Lead Singer

Brother Johnnie Woods
Base Guitar, Background & Fill In

Brother Ronald David
Drummer

In loving Memory of:
Willie (Cat) Thomas, Michael (Mike) Williams, and Reverend Clarence Bailey

Joseph Sleweon & Sons

O ur dad Joseph Sleweon is the best! He is an amazing guy. We are very blessed and thankful that God chose him to be our father. He has taught us so much as we are growing up. He always encourages us as well as our friends. Our dad has always worked very hard to make sure we have the things that we need; clothes, food, and a nice home. Although our dad's work schedule keeps him busy, he always

makes the time to come to the different events we are involved in at school. He also attends our games, concerts, or any event or program that we have. We can always depend on seeing our dad there! He is such a great supporter and encourager for us. We love and appreciate our dad so much, and although he's our dad, he's our Brother In Christ as well.

We Love You, Dad!

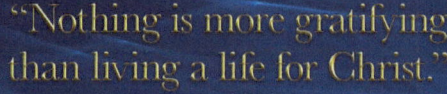

Larry Rice

"Nothing is more gratifying than living a life for Christ."

Growing up, I was inspired by my grandfather, Charles Dobbins. We called him "Paw." He taught Sunday School. I would always tag along with him on Sunday morning. He was a great gardener. He would always plant on Good Friday, and it yielded a good crop. It was a common custom to always plant during this time. We lived next door to each other. When I cut our lawn, I would always cut his. When he passed, I was deeply hurt.

I wanted to become an Aircraft Control and Warning Operator. After graduating from high school, I joined the Air Force for four years. After completing basic training, I went to technical school for the above classification; I was given top-secret security clearance for handling vital and secret information. The job consisted of tracking the speed, height, and location of an aircraft.

I was stationed in Biloxi and Gulfport, Mississippi, at a time when tension was high. James Meridith integrated the University of Mississippi, and we, the military was put on high alert. This was an experience for me. No matter what you are handed in life, put God first. Do not give in to defeat. I encourage my children, grandchildren, and their classmates not to give in. After completing four years of service, I received an honorable discharge.

Nothing has been more gratifying than living a life for Christ, working in outreach ministries, and visiting nursing homes with Deacon Connie Taylor. We would always read inspirational material, sing, and discuss the word of God with them. Deacon Bobbie Stubblefield worked with me in the bread and outreach ministries.

In our clothing ministry, I would help the men find suitable clothing for dress wear, job interviews, leisure, and casual wear. I thank God every day that he has given me the gift of hospitality and administration. I am truly blessed to serve as Superintendent of Sunday School at Liberty Baptist Church. I pray that God will use me wherever and whenever I am needed and always keep me humble as I serve others.

I enjoy waking up every Monday through Thursday listening to morning prayer provided through Liberty Baptist Church Circle of Prayer Line, where we meet other members from state to state. "When praises go up, blessings come down." To God be the Glory, we invite you to join us Monday morning through Thursday at 7:00-7:30 am. Liberty Baptist Church prayer line 712-770-4010, extension 680676#.

Minister Leo Lavender

"The Lord knew what I needed before I asked."

What I like about God is, He sends you directions before you even know you are lost. I am grateful for my dear friend, the late Deacon Darryl Robinson. We worked, for ten years, in the same substance abuse treatment facility. He was the head cook, and I was the assessment counselor. For the first five years, we just greeted each other in passing. He heard that I was into music, so he asked me if I knew anyone who could transfer a cassette to a CD one day. I explained that I could do that for him. I transferred the music from the cassette. It came out perfect, and he was pleased. He tried to pay me, but I told him it was my gift to him. It turned out the Deacon had about two hundred cassettes. He started bringing them two at a time. One day when he was dropping off a cassette tape, he asked my opinion about a situation between him and his wife. When he finished talking, I took him straight to the word of God, explaining that marital love is unconditional. He fired back with, but God is the head of a man, and man is the head of a woman. We shared scripture for about an hour. That afternoon was the start of an intimate spiritual relationship.

I am a minister and debated scripture with other ministers and pastors. None of them had the compassion for God's word that I found in Darryl. He was honest with emotions, genuine, and I trust him with my secrets. You know, the stuff you do not tell anyone

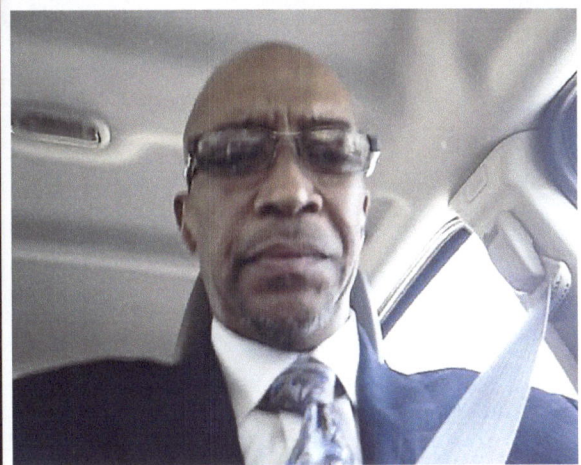

Deacon Darryl Robinson.

but God. He became my prayer and gossip partner. Yeah, I know nobody else gossips. I am just keeping it real. We attended different churches, but two to three times a week, we had bible study in the lunchroom. We edified each other. Our wives became close friends, and occasionally he and his wife would attend our events. Darryl had a kidney transplant around the time I started at the organization. The doctors gave him five years before the new kidney would need replacing. When he passed away from kidney complications, he was in his 12th year with that kidney. The Lord knew what I needed before I asked. I am still feeding on the encouragement he left in me. I thank God for the life of Deacon Darryl Robinson. And by the way, I completed the last two cassettes a month before he passed.

Apostle Leonard Emmons

On April 3, 1973, the doctors said, "If he lives through the night, it will be a miracle." After 6 hours of intense surgery, 6-7 units of blood transfusions, earnest surgical teamwork, patching up an internal mess created by being crushed by the end part of a gigantic steel coil causing major internal injuries. The surgery was to repair a puncture in my inner stomach, removing 18 inches of crushed intestines and reattaching veins on both sides of my abdomen.

After remaining in the hospital for 13 days, I lost 20-25 pounds. I was released from the hospital without any perspective of what my life was going to be like especially since I had been healthy all of my 19 years. The doctor's noted that my good health before the accident, was a major benefit for my recovery. I survived that surgery, and 48 years later, I am still here to testify of God's goodness.

However, there was something else going on that I was not aware of: God was seeking me out. In the follow-up visits to the doctors, they started calling me the "miracle boy." "Miracle boy" has stuck with me all these years. Twelve months later, God had miraculously changed me. Within six months of the accident, I was moved and inspired to read the Bible. As I read the Bible, it was as though God's presence was noticeable, and the Bible's words appeared to be illuminated and jump off the page. Because I was not brought up in church, His presence was like nothing I had ever experienced, and I became addicted to the word of God. I began reading the gospels and was overwhelmed by God's unconditional love. I came to understand that the miracle in April was not an accident but providential.

God started to work on me with my character, attitude, behavior, and habits. He helped me to stop smoking cigarettes which I had been smoking since the age of twelve. He stopped me from cussing and using vulgarity and drinking hard alcohol and hard drugs (even though I continued to drink wine and beer), and smoked marijuana. Finally, he stopped me from looking at and reading porn magazines. He started me to study the Bible and to pray daily.

At the beginning of 1974, I was lead to start fasting with prayer weekly, which I continued throughout my life. I became aware that God was with me even though I had many problems. With this the Lord helped me to deal with pain, with or without pain medication. I also started to believe that all things are possible to those that believe in God's word.

I discovered through fasting and praying that God could keep me and strengthen me. I grew in confidence and faith and further yielded myself to Him using me. In April of 1974 when asked, what role or function I would pursue in the church, I replied that l wanted to preach God's word. However, this was not me because l was an introvert who seldom spoke, and I have been preaching ever since.

BECAUSE OF WHAT GOD DID FOR ME, NOW I HAVE:

- Became a good father to my children and a father figure to nieces, nephews, and siblings.
- Became a role model for my family and led them to Christ.
- Became a role model to church members, community, co-workers, substance abusers within the recovery community.
- By April of 1976, God delivered me totally from all alcohol and drug use.
- He started to use me in 1976 as a bible teacher at the age of "23".

Apostle Leonard Emmons has known Jesus as his savior since 1971, was filled with the Holy Spirit in 1976, has been in public ministry since 1983, ordained in 1985, pastoring since 1988 with an earnest pursuit to raise up believers to fullfil their destiny in ministry call so that the Gospel of the Kingdom will be preached in all the world for a witness unto all the nations ... Matthew 24:14.

He has a degree in Theology, has completed training courses Crusaders Ministries International (Overseer Apostle John Eckhardt and Apostle Coy & Delphine Wade Director of Crusaders Prophetic School), along with training completions at Global Harvest Ministry (JP Wagner Institute for Partical Ministry) & also sessions such as Ministering Spiritual Gifts, Developing Prophetic Ministry, Church Prophetic Teams, Apostolic Church Growth, Miracles Now and Prophetic Deliverance Advanced with Christian International, has been trained to effectively minister in the areas of deliverance and the prophetic, presently is an approved instructor of CIMN to facilitate this training.

As an apostolic and prophetic leader, he has traveled and ministered with teams to St. Lucia and South Africa; has a passion to see the body of Christ "perfected and equipped to do the world of the ministry (of Jesus) Eph. 4: 11-16.

- Since the April 3, 1973 surgery and hospital stay, I have not been hospitalized for anything. God has kept me well.
- I have been privileged to preach the gospel locally, nationally, and Internationally.
- Out of His mercy, Jesus has used me to get people saved, healed, delivered, and restored to God along with many of their families.

Pre-SCRIPTION FOR A GODLY LIFE WITH THE FATHER

- Seek the Kingdom of God. (Matthew 6:33)
- Make Jesus and His Kingdom priority One! (Jude 1:3)
- Spend time with God through prayer and in His word.
- Be filled with the Holy Spirit!! {Luke 24:49, Acts 1:4-5)
- Make repentance a daily priority. (Acts 17:30)
- Make fasting and prayer a weekly priority. Jesus said, "when you fast."
- Talk to others about Jesus.
- Ask God to deliver you from satanic oppression. (Acts 10:38)
- Forgive others so you can be forgiven. (Mark 11:25)
- With God's help, walk in Jove. {I Cor. 13:4-8)
- Bind the enemy in your affairs. {Matthew 18:18-20)
- Embrace the call of God on your life. Everyone is called. (I Cor. 5:18)
- Remember, you have an assignment, Finish Your Course. (I nm. 4:7)
- Intercede and pray for others. (Ezekiel 22:30, James 5:16)
- Ask for the Holy Spirit to help you live daily!! (John 14,15,16)

Elder Marlon Reavy

"What can I say about My Brothers In Christ?"

What can I say about my Brother In Christ/Life Apostle Shon Mitchell?

Matt: 13:11 The mysterious of the kingdom of heaven are revealed through the insight of Shon Mitchell for abundant life of the hearer.

I met this extraordinary man of God the summer of 2017 for the first time and it was a life changing moment for my life as I heard the Word of God like never before from his lips of clay. I had just recently married my Senior Prom date Samantha from Chicago that June after not seeing or communicating with her for over 31 years. We were recommended to visit Apostle Shon's Community called New Covenant Life Kingdom Community located at the time in Virginia Beach by Prophetess Renee Jacob from Chicago who knew him and his lovely wife Prophetess Marie Mitchell from their home town Omaha, Nebraska. That day was an apostolic experience I will never forget. As the prophetic word was spoken over my life and my wife's Samantha life we were drawn to their ministry slowly but surely to be future leaders and help to their ministry and we didn't even know it initially. Apostle Shon affectionately known as "Dad" is a spiritual father, mentor, father, friend, confidant, etc.. He is true man of God who believes being very honest and transparent with his delivery of God's Word to God's people. The way he breaks the Word of God in lament terms that even a child can understand it is so awesome. All the things that I thought I knew in the Word of God was revealed to me Sunday after

APOSTLE SHON A. MITCHELL SR.

Sunday as the Word came forth from Apostle Shon, Prophet Marie or Elder Chris scales would fall off my eyes. He is faithfully busy daily ministering locally and internationally to other communities under New Covenant Life Kingdom Community in Cape Town, Lesotho, Pakistan, and Johannesburg, Africa. He is well known for his apostolic anointing of God's Word and prophetic anointing and many gifts. He is a God-fearing man, loves God's people and he has a very big and caring heart for those in need. We joined the New Life Covenant Kingdom Community in September 2019 shortly after our Mother Iceal Peavy made her transition from earth to heavenly peace with the Lord. As we were making our transition from just being regular church members after 13 weeks of CIP (Community Integrating Process) like a New Member's Course but so much powerful we became shareholders with the ministry. During the pandemic COVID-19 Apostle Shon led the entire community and challenged us to join him in a 40 day fast from things like certain foods,

movies and television programs we use to watch, negative words, etc…over a year's time we started and completed weekly teachings via Zoom, FB Live and in-person services with reduced members during the beginning of COVID 19 we covered The First Creation, The Fallen Creation, The New Creation, Soul Ties, and The Final Creation. It has been a great journey thus far. Apostle Shon also has Shon A Mitchell Ministries which covers several initiatives (services) provided like Financial Peace, Grief Share, BTTB (Better Than the Best) for our young children up to high school, Joshua Generation for our Young Adults, Divorce Care, SYMBIS (Saving Your Marriage Before It Starts), Tyranus Institute, Noah's Company (Men's Ministry) and Daughters of Sarah (Women's Ministry). Apostle Shon has been another spiritual father hand-picked by God just for me who has been a great role model, faithful friend, encourager, prayer warrior and true brother who is trustworthy. He always has an encouraging and powerful/life-changing Word for me, words of wisdom concerning natural and spiritual things. Thank you and Marie for welcoming and accepting Samantha and I into your home, community, and especially your hearts. I am eternally grateful for the covenant connection that God has created between us. You are and will always be my LIFE BROTHER…..thank you for sharpening me with iron over and over again with your love and God's Word!! I love you to life. Thank you for being more than a friend one of your many spiritual sons for eternal life!!

What a blessing it has been to have my brother and true friend Elder Harold Johnson.

He has been faithful in my life these past 8 years. He truly has a deep and personal relationship with our Lord and Savior Jesus Christ. He has always been there for me in just about every season of my life since I have known him. We both were ordained as Elders in October in 2013 at our church in Virginia Beach, VA where we served faithfully in the ministry, men's ministry, church operations and various other areas. He shared so much wisdom as a father, grandfather, friend, true confidant, pre/post marriage counseling and my spiritual Uncle in the Lord.

Elder Harold and his lovely wife Evangelist Mae accepted my new wife Prophetess/ Evangelist Samantha back in June 2017 after we married after last seeing one another 31 years prior. They both were so genuine, very honest and transparent with us and the call that the Lord had on our lives. Uncle Harold and Auntie Mae both were always a phone call, text or visit away as I had experienced persecution in the church from several areas. Instead of telling me to leave or abandon the church and the Lord they encouraged me in the Lord and prayed for me; my strength, forgiveness, restoration, service, humbleness and obedience unto the Lord. If I was wrong they (Uncle and Auntie) would correct me in love and if I was right Uncle Harold would reward me with a holy warm hug, words of encouragement to stay in the race. I was extremely blessed and fortunate to have them both in my life at that time since my biological father had just passed away Dec 2012.

I was seeking a godly father figure, mentor and true friend that I could confide in for morale and godly wisdom support as I was going through a very ugly divorce at the time. We both had a true love and passion for the Lord, His Kingdom people and most importantly the lack of godly men in the church. Throughout my life I had very few men in my entire life that I could call a true friend that I could trust and depend on so I never took his friendship, leadership, prayers and unconditional love for granted. He made my life so much richer by just being there for me through the good, the bad, the ugly, the highs, the lows, and most importantly, the awesome spiritual moments he chose to share with me. Thank you and Auntie from the bottom of my heart for never giving up on me and for accepting me just as I was/I am. Uncle Harold and I were both committed to the Men's Ministry for our church serving at the church and in the community. We could always depend on one another during our Saturday monthly men's meeting, men's praise team practices and men's day Sundays that we had to lead the church in praise and worship. Whenever I needed an encouraging word he was always there to give me a Word from the

MARLON & HAROLD

Lord in the Bible. Always a scripture/Word to live by.

We saw God move miraculously and answer so many of our prayers while serving together in ministry. It would always be such a powerful and anointed time of prayer whenever we would get together to pray and worship in person or on the phone/text. I love to go to God in prayer with Uncle Harold because we were always united and focused on defeating our enemies in those moments. That meant the world to me because, in God's remarkable presence, our hearts were overflowing with joy and expectation of how our Heavenly Father was going to answer our prayers. Uncle Harold was not only my prayer partner and mentor, but he was my brother, friend, protector, confidant, one of my biggest supporters, and praise partner.

I could always count on Uncle Harold to do the right thing and be ready to give the devil a black eye at the moment whenever I asked him to pray "for" me or "with" me. He has such an incredible giving and supportive heart. It is such an honor and joy not only to have him as my covenant brother, male mentor but an amazingly loving Brother In Christ. Elder Harold Johnson served the U.S. Government as a Civil Service employee for over 40 years and retired and still serving as a Contractor for the Govt. He and his lovely wife Auntie Mae continue to be passionate servants for the body of Christ actively participating at their current ministry. On July 27, 2019 Elder Harold received the "Bachelor of Theological Diplomacy" Degree from C4GD School of Diplomatic Leadership in Virginia Beach, VA. where Apostle Burnell T. Williams serves as Chancellor. Elder Harold is a committed man of God, dedicated husband, father, grandfather, great-grandfather, and uncle.

I Corinthians 16:13-14 says "Be watchful, stand firm in the faith, act like men, be strong. Let all that you do be done in love." And Jeremiah 29:11 says "For I know the plans I have for you," declares the LORD, "plans to prosper you and not to harm you, plans to give you hope and a future." Thank God for your true friendship down through the years, for your unconditional love, constant prayers and for always supporting and believing in me. Iron truly does sharpen iron. So grateful that the Lord placed you permanently in my life. You have made your mark on my life with God's imprint, plan, purpose and design in mind. Your loving nephew always!!

What can I say about my Brother In Christ/Life, Pastor Perry Hill?

3 John1:5 (MSG) says it best. "Dear friend, when you extend hospitality to Christian brothers and sisters, even when they are strangers, you make the faith visible."

Our friendship is and was God-ordained from the very beginning. We have only known each other less than 12 months after our wives connected last summer via our Chicago Prophetess mentor Renee Jacob to support an Intercessory Prayer call and Pastor Perry Hill and his lovely wife Evangelist Angeline Hill requested assistance with Zoom call training since we were at the beginning months of the pandemic COVID-19 which helped support social distancing for future church services at their church Rivers of Life C.O.G.I.C. So my beloved wife (Prophetess/Evangelist Samantha) being who she is in the spirit of excellence began to train both Pastor and Evangelist Hill and their leadership team. We finally got a chance to meet them both last fall of 2020 after they invited us to spend the weekend with them at their lovely home in Burlington, NC. They didn't know us from a can of paint but they welcomed us into their homes as they very own son and daughter immediately. It was as though we had/have known them both our whole life. Nothing but the unconditional love of God. Pastor Perry Hill affectionately known as "Papa" has been a true brother, mentor, friend, confident, and a wise father figure to Samantha and I both. He always has an encouraging Word for me/us, words of wisdom concerning natural and spiritual things and he and Mom Evangelist Angeline both accept Samantha and I as their spiritual children in the Lord. Both of our biological fathers are no longer alive here on earth but we have found a true father in Pastor Hill.

PASTOR PERRY HILL

Pastor Hill encouraged me in a big way as I was overcoming from senior leadership challenges after serving for 9 plus years at my former church in Virginia on the ministerial staff. He gave me some really good Godly wisdom as he had personally experienced it once as a Pastor. It really helped my healing and recovering process and most importantly my forgiveness and complete restoration from old ungodly sold ties. He is a true leader who loves God, his wife, his family, his friends, his church congregation, and God's kingdom. We both served our country in the military for over 20 plus years faithfully as well as served the Lord during our years in service for our country. We both have God fearing and praying wives not to mention they are some beautiful and virtuous women of God. We both love encouraging and building men of God and we both love and believe the power of prayer. He is the loving Pastor of the congregation at Rivers of Life C.O.G.I.C.

he established Lifeline International Prayer Center back in 2014 and is the Co-Host of Sip –n – Chat with Angeline which was birthed during COVID-19. We are eternally connected forever and I am so grateful for my LIFE BROTHER…..

The word says "Iron sharpens Iron" and that he did. I love you to life. Thank you for being more than a friend your spiritual son for eternal life!!

Pastor Morris Patterson

"I love him as a brother."

M y first time meeting Pastor Princeton H. Holt was as a senior in high school at Oakwood Academy in Huntsville, Alabama. He was matriculating at Oakwood University as a senior theology student.

I was inspired by Princeton because of his deep level of commitment and dedication to Jesus Christ. After further studies at Andrews University, Pastor Holt accepted the call to evangelistic and Pastoral duties in the South Atlantic part of the United States.

While serving well over 40 years, Pastor Holt showed continual evidence of his calling to kingdom building by baptizing thousands of souls and planting three churches. He is also the founder of a global radio station,

PASTOR PRINCETON H. HOLT

Dawn Christian Fellowship Community Church, and now serves as founder and CEO of Agents of Change International. This movement is designated to impact adverse culture influences wherever they are found.

Additionally, Pastor Holt is Pastor of Timothy Baptist Church in Brooklyn, NY.

Princeton is a lifelong friend, confidant, mentor, spiritual advisor, prayer partner and he continually challenges me to sharpen my gifts and skills to their highest potential. He also has written a relevant book for these times "What turns innocent kids into ruthless killers." I love him as a brother and thank God for putting him into my life for such a time as this.

Pastor Richard Kennedy

"My Brother In Christ and friend..."

M y Brother In Christ and friend since childhood is Brother George Akins Jr. Brother George has and still is a great asset to my life. He has been there for me through my ups and my downs. When my precious wife, Pastor Artice Kennedy Transitioned this pass year, Brother George was there to pray me through, talk me through to the place that began my healing process.

There is so much I could say about George, but to make a long story short, whenever I need him, wherever I need him and whatever I need him for, spiritually, mentally, emotionally, and financially My Brother In Christ, George was and is there for me.

GEORGE AKINS JR.

Pastor Robert L. Cottoner

"Coming up on the rough side of the mountain."

I was born on August 3, 1945, in Durham, North Carolina, to Gertrude and Robert Daly Cottoner. I was one of eight children born to a mother who worked in the homes of white families as a domestic worker and a father who worked in construction. As a young boy, I cleaned houses until I graduated high school, but in 1962 I received my calling into the ministry. I served under the leadership of Pastor C.D. Martin at Oak Grove Missionary Baptist Church in Madisonville, KY, and as an associate pastor for Pastor Thomas E. Matchen at New Mount Zion Missionary Baptist Church in Depoy, KY. In 1963 I received another call for service in the United States Army and retired honorably with the classification of Master Sgt- E-8. I married my wife Jonell in 1967 and raised six children. One child, Keith, passed

at age 18. On July 31, 1985, illness fell upon Oak Grove's pastor, Pastor C.D. Martin, and I felt that my lifetime church family needed my service far greater than the military. I retired and accepted the position of Pastor in November of 1985 and held the position at Oak Grove Missionary Baptist Church for 36 years.

During the 36 years of pastoring, I focused on building a new fellowship hall and church building. I used the youth as a catalyst for bringing others into God's Kingdom with a youth bible ministry and a youth choir. I became a member of the African American Coalition. They aid the youth by giving away school supplies, holding youth seminars, offering youth basketball and sports activities, and school mentoring for high school. I am also a member of the Minister, Deacon, and

Laymen group that helps with youth revival, youth fellowship, and community-wide revival and outreach. This organization sponsors two scholarships for area high schools and one adult scholarship. As one of the board of directors for Bethel Outreach Ministries, we offer assistance to families, food baskets, and a self-help ministry for women. I took the lead in our community against social injustice and serves willing to all who come in need. Cottoner Lawn Care Services often employs men that society has given up on because God has called me to seek and help those who have lost their way. That is how I show that I am a Brother In Christ.

Robert "Bob" Leavell

"Men in my life."

I am the brother of Sister Shirley Rice, and she asked me to write something about myself. It has taken too long to get this started. The more I thought about what I was going to say, the more I realize that there is only one place I can begin. And that is home.

I am the fourth oldest of 10 children. Our parents were strict but very loving. We were a family of touchers and hugged a lot. Even in bad times, we hugged. We cared for and looked after each other. Even to this day, there is nothing that I would not do for my family. Our parents were church-going people. You could bet that I would be in church for Sunday school morning service and BTU on Sunday. I am not complaining. Oh no! What I found at church was something that I would not have found anywhere else in my early life. And that

is Christ. I wish I could say that I was a perfect Christian. I was not. But I have a perfect God. My God placed good men in my life that helped to shape me.

Let us start with my dad. Dad was a Deacon at church. I remember listening to him pray in his quiet times. Some of the best prayers I ever heard were from dad. My dad was a hardworking man. He worked in underground coal mines for over 40 years. Dad hardly ever missed a day of work. And when he got home from work, he would have me help him in the garden. Something that I liked doing. My mom said that I got my work ethic from him. My dad also taught me patience, even though I did not realize that at the time. He would show me how to do different tasks. Things like teaching me how to do carpentry work. I do not know how many pieces of wood I messed up or how many nails I bent. He kept working with me until I became a man and father. When I would work with my son on different projects, it would be difficult because he was slow getting what I was trying to teach him. Then I would remember how patient my dad was with me and how he would allow me to make mistakes until I got it right.

Then there was my friend Allan Gilmore. We were neighbors and classmates. Sometimes, when I would visit his home, his dad, a preacher, would read Bible stories to us—talking about God and his goodness. I enjoyed being around this man of God in my young life. I also enjoyed being around his son. Later in life, he became a preacher. Could this man sing. We had lots of good times together, and we joined the Army about the same time. We both went to Viet Nam. By the Grace of God, we both returned home safe. The stories that we live to tell. A few years ago, he was called home. I really do miss him.

Let me tell you about my cousins Ray & Jerry Hopson. They are strong men of God. When we were in our early twenties, I was reading this book on angels. It was an excellent book to read. I told Ray about this book, and he asked if he could read it. It did influence him. Later Ray said to me that after reading this book, he decided to go into the ministry. I realize then how God could use anyone to spread the Gospel.

PASTOR ROBERT L. COTTONER

Another very influential man in my life is Reverend Robert L. Cottoner, my Pastor. Pastor Cottoner has been in my life for quite some time now. We have prayed together, worshiped together, and even sang together. We have fought many battles together. We have stood on the front lines as warriors for God. It was an honor to serve with him. Pastor Cottoner has been preaching for over 40 years now. I am sure that he has seen it all. He has been an excellent teacher.

I have learned much in my life. When I was 12 years old, my friends and I went swimming in a coal stripper pit. After 30 minutes of swimming, I got severe leg cramps. I went down and came up three times. The last time I did not come up. I took a deep breath and crawled on the bottom until I reached the shore. It was not my time, and I felt lucky. I have seen much death in my life. When I went to Viet Nam and returned home, I said I was one of the lucky ones. I was working as a locomotive Engineer in Chicago in 1999. I was doing a temporary transfer. I was running a loaded coal train from Madison yard to Toledo, Ohio, one late night. It was very dark and foggy.

I was running on a slow approach signal and was looking for a stop signal. The conductor said there was no signal ahead of us. Experience told me there was. I stopped the train. I got off the engine and began looking for a signal. It was so foggy you could cut it with a knife. I walked no more than ten feet, and there it was—a signal with a burned-out bulb. Five minutes later, I heard a westbound train blowing at crossings. If I had not stopped, there would have been a head-on collision. I did not say I was lucky this time because I had learned that luck had nothing to do with my good fortune. I had been giving credit to something that had nothing to do with my good fortune. Glory be to God. He had been walking with me all my life. His grace and mercy is the only reason that I am here today. The only reason that I can write this to you. May his blessing be upon all of you this day and always.

Pastor Royce F. Thompson Sr.

"Men it's time to get up and claim your inheritance"

Reference scripture: JOSHUA 1:2-18

Joshua gives an Old Testament example of what is expected of us in the New Testament. Today many Christian men are "MENTALLY PREPARED" to enter their Promised Land and receive the inheritance their Father gave them before the foundation of the world. Many of the men today are not walking in the place where God can work through them to enforce what Jesus has already obtained for them. And that is total and complete victory over Satan and his demonic kingdom. One of the primary reasons why we are not "doing the works Jesus did," and I am not even talking about the "greater," is because we do not see ourselves as God and Jesus see us. The Holy Spirit brought this point home to me as I was reading the first chapter of the book of Joshua. Joshua was "mentally unprepared" to lead Israel to the Promised Land even though he knew that he would be the one to lead after Moses. That is why you have to be transformed by the renewing of your mind through Christ Jesus.

Now, in verse 1 of Joshua chapter 2, Joshua is Israel's leader. But he still has not come to grips with Moses' death. The period of mourning was over, and Joshua had not taken charge of Israel. Joshua knew that he would be Moses' successor; Israel even knew it. But now the day has arrived. It was time for Joshua to do what he had been prepared to do – what he had been called to do – what he was capable of doing.

In verse 2, the Lord has to remind Joshua that Moses is dead and that he is now looking to Joshua to stand up and be the man. When the Lord says, "Moses, my servant is dead," it is as if he is taking Joshua by the shoulders and shaking him to get his attention. "Moses, my servant is dead, Joshua!" He is not coming back! I have buried him! NOW GET UP! ARISE (stand up and be the man)! God may have to do that to us. In John 14:12 KJV, Jesus says, "Verily, verily I say unto you, He that believeth on me, the works that I do, ye shall do also; and greater than these shall he do; because I go unto my father." In this New Testament example, God is telling us that, "Jesus, my beloved son, the obedient son, the anointed son is no longer here. He is gone! Now get up. Stand up and be the man I have called you to be. My people need you. I need you." Do you see this? Like Joshua, we have a job to do, a job that we are capable of doing. God is not going to give you a job that he has not prepared you for; He will not send you anywhere His Grace can not keep you.

So, to get up and claim your inheritance, you have to BE DECISIVE (Joshua 1:2-6)... (v2). You cannot live in the past - God has given you an assignment; you have to make a decision based on where you're going, not where you've been. You have to make a decision based on where God is taking you. You have to change your thinking and change your thought process. The hardest thing for the human to do is to think. One day I talked to a young man in my office about changing our thinking, and I told him, "We are great at reacting, but we are poor at thinking. We do our best thinking when we are trying to get out of the situation we got in for reacting." How many of you were in a situation you knew you had no business getting in but was not thinking, and then you got in it, and now you said let me think about how I will get out

of this? We have to put ourselves in better positions to make wiser decisions!

Secondly, to get up and claim your inheritance, you have to BE DISCIPLINED (Joshua 1:7-13). God is not a "God of compromise," he does not make negotiations; either you are all in or you are not! He tells Joshua for the third time be strong and courageous. When we are following God, we have to be confident, at peace, and focused on the Word of God! Your victory requires complete obedience, and any deviation can bring forfeiture of the prize.

Lastly men, you have to BE DETERMINED (Joshua 1:14-17)...(14-16). Do not allow the details to derail you from reaching the prize that God has for you. Determination will lead to domination; if you are focused on something, you will conquer it. You have to make a visible and verbal commitment to follow through with God's instruction (lip service will not work anymore!)

In verse 17, because of their Decision, Discipline, and Determination, they were able to experience victory in their battle. Because they did not get caught up in the leadership change, and they followed through with the instructions of God. When you put your trust in the plan and not in the person, you will have victory. In verse 18, not only were they determined to follow God's plan to the letter, but they also made up in their minds to not let the haters stop them! Listen, men, and listen good. If you are going to win the battle, you have to learn to eliminate the haters in your life. Not with weapons, but with your praise to God! The reason you should rejoice when the haters hate is because, haters never hate on somebody that is not doing anything. Haters only hate on folks that are doing something. And you ought to get a delight when they hate because that lets you know that you are on the right path, and God is getting ready to do something great! The Bible says in 1 Corinthians 2:9, "No eye has seen, no ear heard, and no mind has imagined what God has prepared for those who love him." So to all men and fathers, it is time for us to GET UP and get in a position to claim our inheritance and everything that God has in store for us. So that we can be the men, He has created us to be!

Pastor Royce F. Thompson, Sr.
New Friendship Missionary Baptist Church
1545 Waite Street Gary, IN 46404
219-949-4279
Personal Email: royce_thompson@yahoo.com
Church Email: newfriendshipmbc@sbcglobal.net
Website: www.newfriendshipgary.org
Facebook:
@Royce F. Thompson, Sr.
@NewFriendshipGary
Instagram:
@PastorRFT
@NFMBC1958
YouTube:
@New Friendship Missionary Baptist Church

Sam Haymon

"God blessed me with an amazing dad."

A brother is someone you share a special bond with, someone you can talk to about almost anything. Someone who you know has your back, and you have his—someone you can trust.

I consider my father to be My Brother In Christ. When I think of my father, I think of strength, wisdom, and leadership. As a young kid, I was blessed to have a father who exhibited all those characteristics and more. My father has always been there for his family. He has always been extremely hard-working, dedicated, and stern with a lot of stick-to-it-ive-ness. He instilled in my siblings and I the same values. I am the youngest son of William Haymon Jr. Being

WILLIAM HAYMON JR.

the youngest son of six kids, you get to see a lot, and I took it all in. I always admired how my father would juggle work, being a husband, a great father, and still finding the time to coach my brothers and I in baseball.

I find my father to be brilliant. Although quiet, he somehow figured out how to maneuver through life, raise his family and make it look easy. He has blessed so many people along the way. I remember hearing stories about him walking in a blizzard to get my brother a pair of boots. Another time he gave a stranger the coat off his back, because the man was standing in the cold without a coat.

There are countless ways my father has

impacted my life. When my father's car broke down and was in the shop, he would get up extra early each morning and walk for miles and miles to work to provide for his family, and he would get there on time. Another thing about my father, he is a stickler about getting to where you need to be on time. I have never witnessed my father call off work in all the years I was growing up. My father is truly the perfect example of a positive role model, leader, and good provider.

Today I am a married man of 13 years with four children of my own, and I see a lot of my father in me. Sometimes when I am at work, people will look at me confused and say, "Man, why are you working so hard?" I smile and say, "My ole man is a great example," and to this day, I have never been late for work. My father and I share a special bond, much like a brother. I thank God for my father, whom I respect to the utmost, and I can say he is my Brother In Christ.

Sherman Peavy

"I thank God for my three awesome brothers."

I am a very blessed man to have three awesome brothers. I have so many precious memories growing up in Gary, Indiana in a loving Christian home. My parents Samuel and Julia Peavy made sure we attended church. On Sundays there was Sunday School and Worship Service, during the week we went to bible study and choir rehearsal. On the weekend we did maintenance at church such as cleaning and cutting the grass, etc. All three of my brothers and I loved music, we had our own little band. I played the guitar, Michael the keyboard, Calvin and Gerry played the drums. We loved going fishing with our dad and uncles. I could go on and on about all the amazing memories, but I'll just share a little about each of my magnificent brothers.

Gerry at a very young age always wanted

GERRY PEAVY

to preach, on Saturdays while doing chores at church he would stand behind the Pastor's pulpit and do his made-up sermons. My siblings Sharon, Wilma, Calvin. Michael and I would sit and listen to him. I must admit, some of his messages were really good and his favorite song to sing was and still is Victory Is Mine. Well Gerry did not become a pastor when he grew up, he worked as a custodian at Horace Mann High School. Gerry loved his job, loves helping others and he truly loves our Lord and Savior Jesus Christ. He is my brother and one of my best friends!

Calvin served 20 years of active Naval

CALVIN PEAVY

MICHAEL PEAVY

service assigned to: The Naval Administrative Command Great Lakes, Illinois, the U.S. Naval Hospital in Memphis, Tennessee, U.S. Naval Air Facility Sigonella, Sicily, the U.S. Naval Air Technical Training Center Virginia Beach, VA, Fighter Squadron 143, Early Airborne Warning Squadron 122, deployed aboard the aircraft carriers U.S.S. Dwight D. Eisenhower CVN 69, U.S.S. Forrestal CVN 60, and U.S.S. Theodore Roosevelt CVN 71. He retired having attained the rank of Senior Chief Petty Officer. Calvin served as a Captain in the R.O.T.C. program while attending Roosevelt High School which led to him pursuing a military career. Upon retiring from the military, Calvin worked for Pepsi Cola as a Merchandiser and Route Salesman, and Federal Express as an Aircraft Offload crew member and forklift operator. Calvin subsequently became a business owner for 25 years. From starting work at age 10 delivering newspapers to celebrating 5 years in retirement, he is still in search of new ideas, challenges and adventures. Calvin has always been very mature, a impeccable dresser and business minded. He would budget, save his money, and teach us to do the same. I could go on and on about Calvin's wisdom and excellence, but this would turn into a book, so I will stop here.

Michael served in the United States Marine Corps from 1983 to 1987. Stationed at Marine Corps Recruit Depot San Diego, CA, Camp Del Mar, CA, Marine Corps Air Station in Cherry Point, NC, Marine Corps Base Camp Butler in Okinawa, Japan and Camp Pendleton, CA. Michael was honorably discharged at the rank of Corporal, and he thanks God for everything that he experienced. After returning home Michael and I would get together when time permitted to make music like old times. Michael on the keyboard and me on the guitar. I must say that we have made some really good beats together. Michael not only plays the keyboard, but his voice is soothing to the ear. He sings at weddings, funerals, etc. He really connects with people through his incredible voice. We both enjoy writing songs and making beats. When Michael retires and we have more time to spend making music, our songs will speak for themselves!

I thank Michael and Calvin for their love, dedication, and service to our Country. I am so very proud of all three of my amazing brothers, each one of them reminds me of my dad. My dad loved Our Lord and Savior Jesus Christ, his family, friends, and others. He was a hard worker, a giver and always ready to lend a helping hand or bless a person in need. This describes my loving brothers! I am honored and blessed to call each of them brother and My Brothers In Christ!

Samuel   Stephen   Christopher

The Stewarts

Our mother raised us, brothers three. She raised us to be all we could be.

She did not bring us up in church, but she taught us to always KNOW GOD AND TO PUT HIM FIRST.

Our mother raised us to be good men, broad and strong. She taught us how to forgive, turn the other cheek, to have faith, and move on.

People say a woman can not raise a man but by the grace of God she did it…Three of us, three very good men, praising God for our lives looking out for each other through thick and thin.

She would say you will have to pay for the things you do in this life, so be good to all people all of your life.

God fearing men is what she raised us to be, saying our prayers and allowing God to help her mold us brothers three.

She raised us not to be men of the street, but to be kind hearted and to listen and to think before we speak.

She said, "You are all grown now and into the hands of God I have placed you to be men of God and to never give into despair or defeat."

She held our hands until we were grown and she said remember to always keep God in our homes.

She gave us the task to be good men all our lives, she taught us to get married, to be good to our children, and good husbands to our wives.

We are THREE BROTHERS, brothers for life; God fearing brothers and TRUE BROTHERS IN CHRIST.

William Haymon Jr.

"I thank God for my dad."

My father is My Brother In Christ. I remember when I was a little boy, my father was my baseball coach. He taught me how to become a team player. How to work hard and even how to lose a game with dignity. The lessons I learned playing baseball I used all through my life.

Growing up, one of my dad's favorite things to do is go fishing and hunting. Fishing is so relaxing and serene. I enjoyed fishing and hunting with my dad. I can remember driving to Dyersburg, Tennessee with my dad and we would hunt on Thanksgiving morning. At the time it seemed like a fun thing to do, but now, I cannot imagine myself driving a n y w h e r e to hunt on Thanksgiving, but it was a good experience and memories spent with my dad.

Daddy loves the Lord and he raised me with good values. I thank GOD for my dad. He helped raise me to be the man I am today. That is why my dad is My Brother In Christ.

WILLIAM HAYMON JR. (L) & SR. (R)

WILLIAM HAYMON SR.